For Nicola

AT

To Felix and Maria

CM

First North American Edition 1992

First published in 1992 by ABC, All Books for Children,
a division of The All Children's Company Ltd.,
33 Museum Street, London WC1A 1LD

ISBN 0-316-85626-6

Library of Congress Catalog Card Number 91-58608

Library of Congress Cataloging-in-Publication information is available.

10 9 8 7 6 5 4 3 2 1

Published simultaneously in Canada
by Little, Brown & Company (Canada) Limited

Printed in Hong Kong

The

Tapestry

Cats

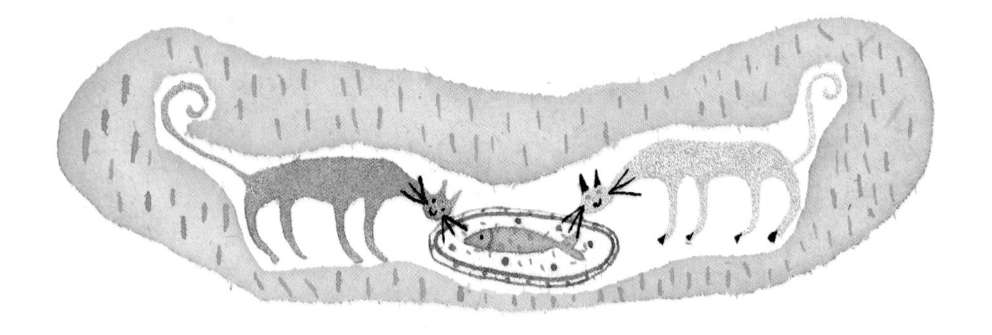

Written by Ann Turnbull ✤ Illustrated by Carol Morley

Little, Brown and Company
Boston Toronto London

Once upon a time there was a princess. She was six years old and she lived in a castle with her mother, the Queen, who always knew what was best for her.

The Queen knew it was best for her daughter to look and behave like a princess at all times, so the princess wore stiff brocade dresses and scratchy tiaras and she was not allowed to jump in puddles or keep pets.

The princess didn't talk much because the Queen always answered for her. Once a duchess asked her what she liked doing best. The Queen replied, "She likes having dancing lessons." So the duchess never knew that the princess preferred reading. Once an uncle asked her what she wanted for Christmas. The Queen replied, "She wants embroidered socks and a yellow petticoat." So the uncle never knew that the princess really wanted a cat.

The princess had no one to play with, so she often wandered alone around the castle, looking at the tapestries that hung on the walls.

These tapestries were old and dusty, and the colors were faded, but the princess liked them because they were full of people and animals.

There were knights in armor riding on horses; princesses who fed unicorns or played harps; ships sailing on choppy seas; dolphins and mermaids.

And there were cats.

The cats were in an upstairs room called the Tower Room. Tapestries hung on two of the walls. One showed a sunny garden with stiff hedges and a lawn scattered with buttercups. A lady sat under a trellis of roses, reading a book, and on her lap was a cat: a big golden tabby cat, embroidered in yellow and cream and glinting gold thread. The princess knew that he was a lazy, friendly cat, as warm as honey and as heavy as sleep. She pretended he was her cat, and she called him Gold.

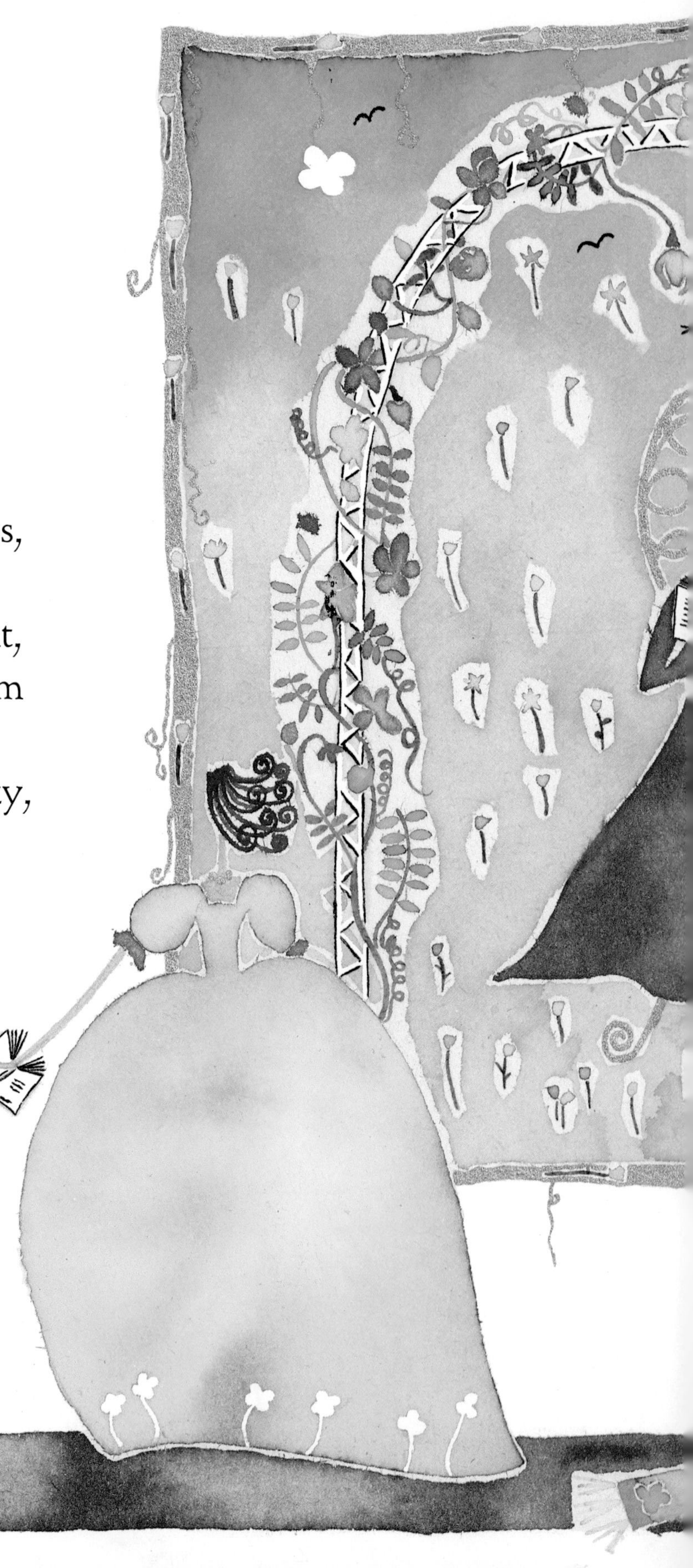

On the opposite wall was the same garden at night. A full moon shone, silvering the arbor, which seemed empty. But when the princess looked closely, down low, by the feet of the lady's chair, she could see a pair of eyes catching the moonlight. A little cat was there: a silver-gray tabby cat, embroidered in black and gray and glinting silver thread. And the princess knew that this was a hunting cat, as secret as moonlight and as quick as thought. She pretended she was her cat, and she called her Silver.

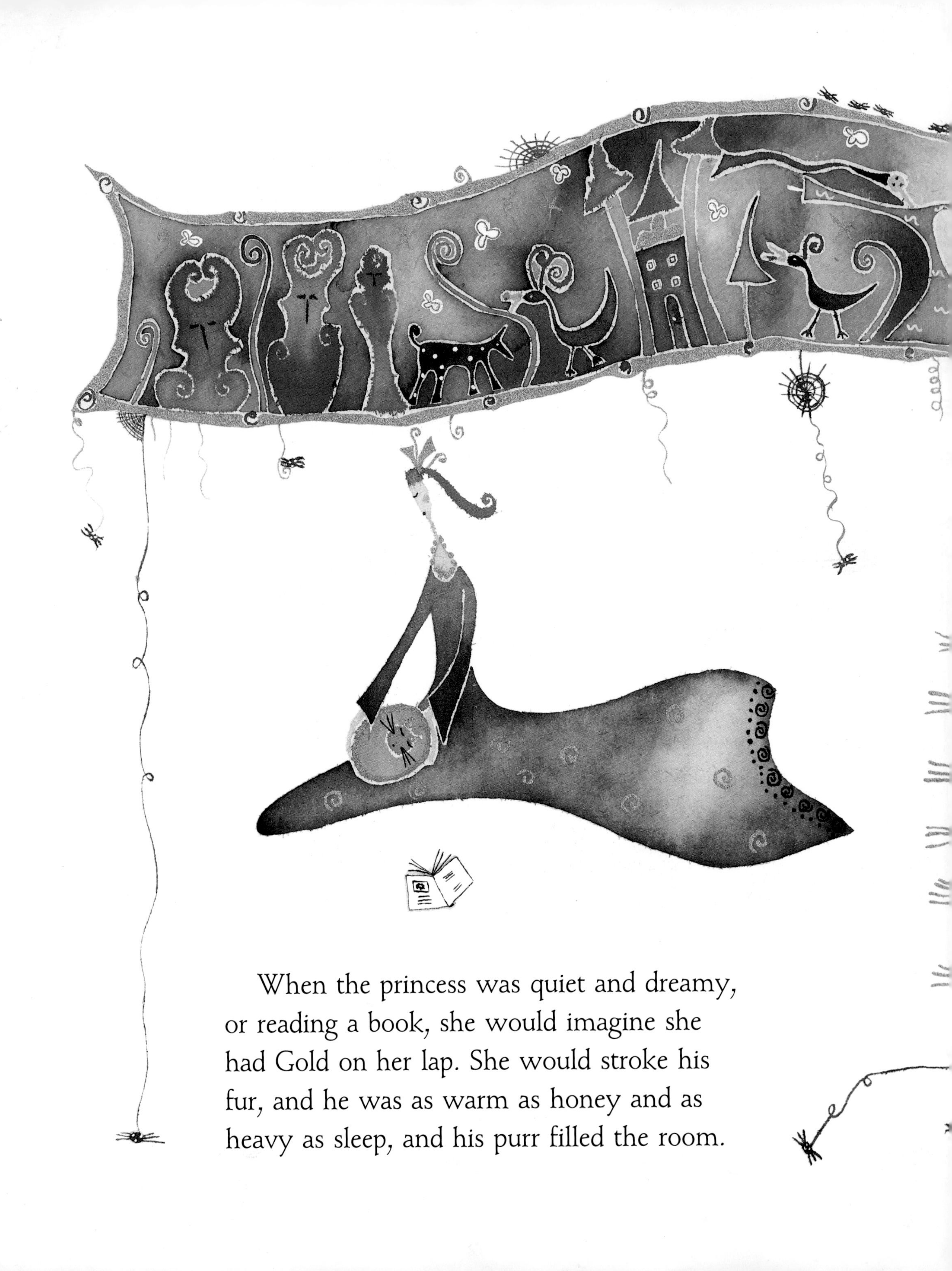

When the princess was quiet and dreamy, or reading a book, she would imagine she had Gold on her lap. She would stroke his fur, and he was as warm as honey and as heavy as sleep, and his purr filled the room.

When the
princess was playful,
running and hiding, she
would imagine she had Silver
with her.

They would play hide-and-seek together all over the castle. But Silver was as secret as moonlight and as quick as thought, and she never let the princess catch her.

On the princess's seventh
birthday her mother organized
a party and invited her
Fairy Godmother.

The princess was given a new tiara, a necklace of rubies, a clockwork bird and a casket full of pearls.

"And what would you like from me?" asked the Fairy Godmother. She smiled at the princess as if she guessed all her thoughts.

The princess knew what she wanted. She opened her mouth, but before she could speak the Queen replied, “Gold and silver. That’s what she wants. Gold and silver.”

The princess's heart leaped. Her eyes opened wide. "*Yes!*" she said. "That *is* what I want."

The Queen smiled at her sensible daughter. The Fairy Godmother waved her wand, and said, "Your wish is granted. Run upstairs and find it." And she winked.

The princess
ran straight to
the Tower Room.

There they were. Gold and Silver. Real cats. Gold was basking in a pool of sunlight. Silver ran and twined around the princess's ankles. The princess knelt to stroke them and Silver sprang up, quick as thought, onto her lap, while Gold pressed his head against her hand. Their purring filled the room.

Of course the Queen was not pleased. She said, "What your Fairy Godmother needs is a new wand." But the princess knew there was nothing wrong with the old one.

And in time the Queen came to like Gold and Silver, and she always knew what was best for them. "What those cats want," she would say, "is salmon flavored with fennel." And she was right.

She was still often wrong about what the princess wanted. But the princess learned to speak up for herself and the Queen learned to say, "Well, dear child, if you insist . . ."

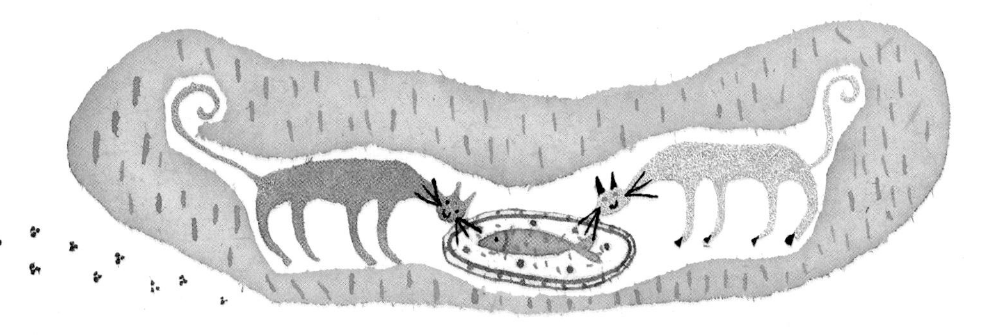

Only the upstairs
chambermaid complained.

She said, "What those tapestries need is moth-proofing. There are holes in two of them as big as cats."